· DEDICATED TO ALL THE ·

SUPERSTAR KIDS

TOGETHER YOU MAKE THIS WORLD A BETTER PLACE

"I exist as I am, that is enough."

In a galaxy filled with stars, the brightest ones, born right here on earth, are our very own

SUPERSTARS!

Let's take a trip to learn about their

SUPERPOWERS!

Hi, my name is Emily.
I've learned I have ADHD.
What have I learned about me?
Well, I have special superpowers,
let me help you see.

I dance to my own drum,
because routine makes me bored.
I like to move and play constantly,
but also need time to withdraw.

My superpower is wisdom,
beyond my years in age.
But what really makes me special,
is how I can break out of a cage.

My heart is so SO big,
it wants to explode with love.
I can't be taught the "normal" way,
because my soul is from above.

You can't put me in a circle,
or in a triangle, or in a box,
as I'm the only one I know
who is cleverer than a fox.

To you I might seem too busy,
to you I might act a little odd;
but you see I am the imperfectly perfect,
most special child from God.

I am my own person,
my very own me.
I AM THE BIGGEST SUPERSTAR
I know, special and unique.

Hi, my name is Lexia,
I've learned I have dyslexia.
What have I learned about me?
Well, I have special superpowers,
let me help you see.

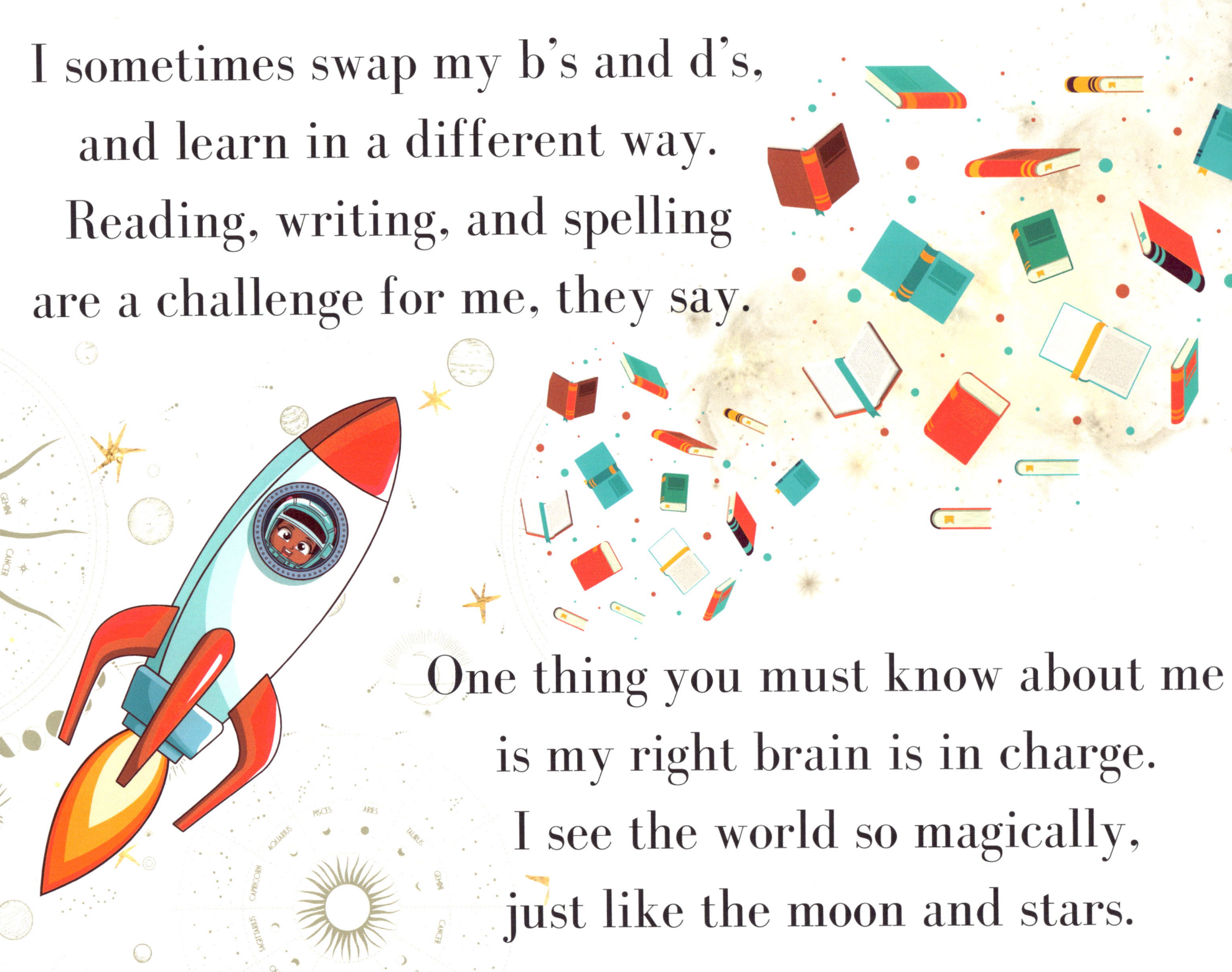

I sometimes swap my b's and d's,
and learn in a different way.
Reading, writing, and spelling
are a challenge for me, they say.

One thing you must know about me
is my right brain is in charge.
I see the world so magically,
just like the moon and stars.

I can get a little frustrated
in some of the mainstream schools;
but even though others soar with work,
I like to break the rules.

This doesn't mean I'm less than you,
I know I have such wisdom.
It just allows me the space and time
to challenge all our systems.

To you I might seem a little different,
to you I might act a little odd;
but you see I am the imperfectly perfect,
most special child from God.

I am my own person,
my very own me.
I AM THE BIGGEST SUPERSTAR
I know, special and unique.

Hi, my name is Griffin.
I've learned I have Autism.
What have I learned about me?
Well, I have special superpowers,
let me help you see.

I can be sensitive and fragile,
emotions up and down;
but when you get to know me,
you'll see my special crown.

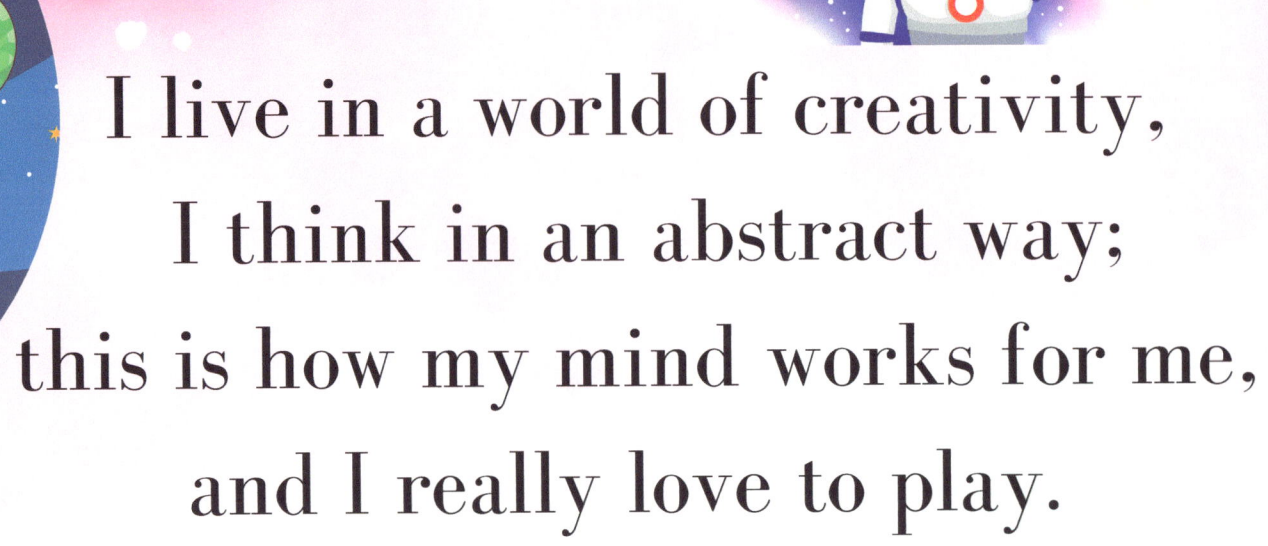

I live in a world of creativity,
I think in an abstract way;
this is how my mind works for me,
and I really love to play.

My superpower is loving,
everyone and everything.
But what really makes me special,
is how I teach you things.

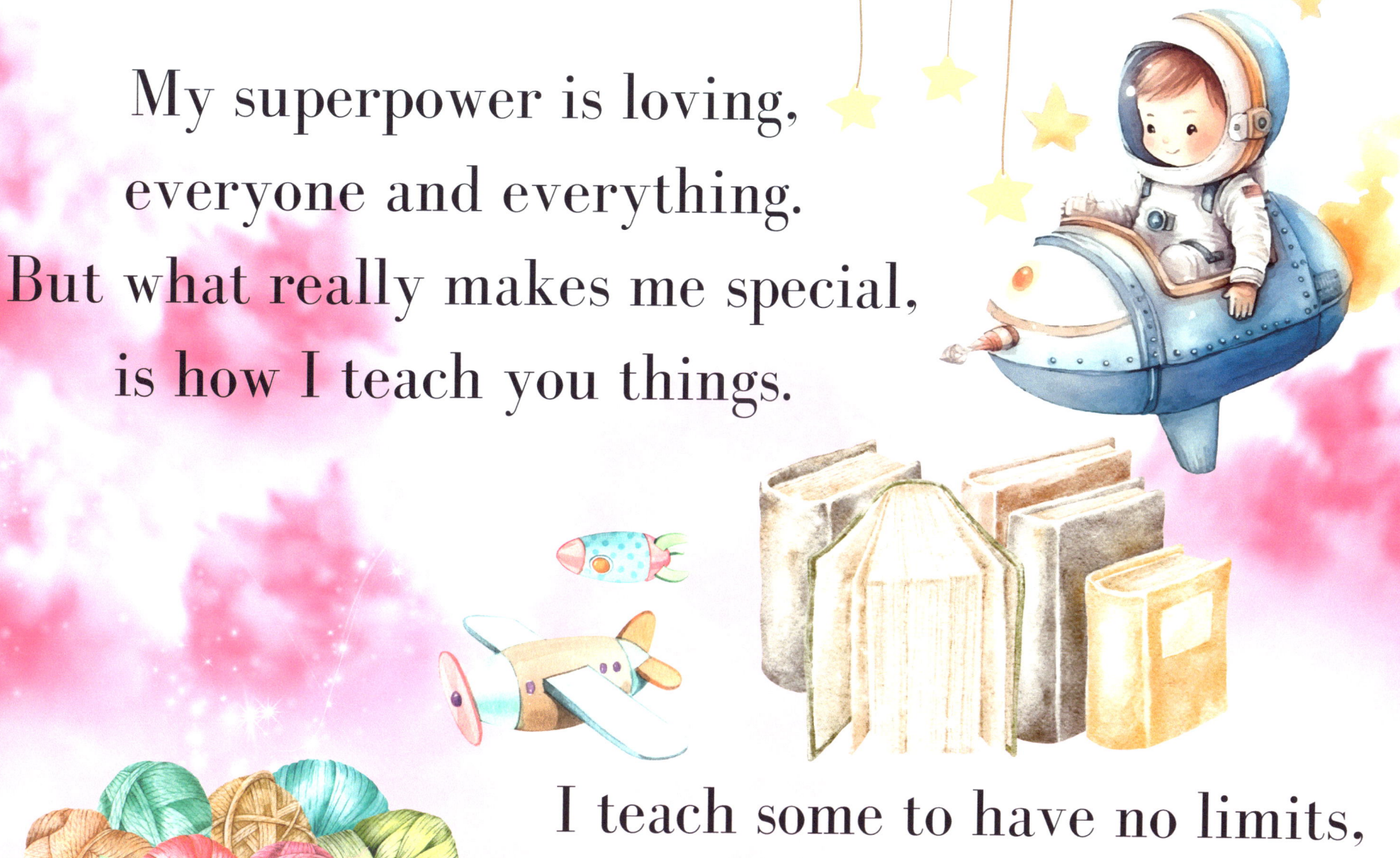

I teach some to have no limits,
and others to have no strife.
I teach most to have more patience,
but to all, I teach you about life.

To you I might look a little different,
to you I might act a little odd;
but you see I am the imperfectly perfect,
most special child from God.

I am my own person,
my very own me.
I AM THE BIGGEST SUPERSTAR
I know, special and unique.

Hi, my name is Sinjen.
I've learned I have Down Syndrome.
What have I learned about me?
Well, I have special superpowers,
let me help you see.

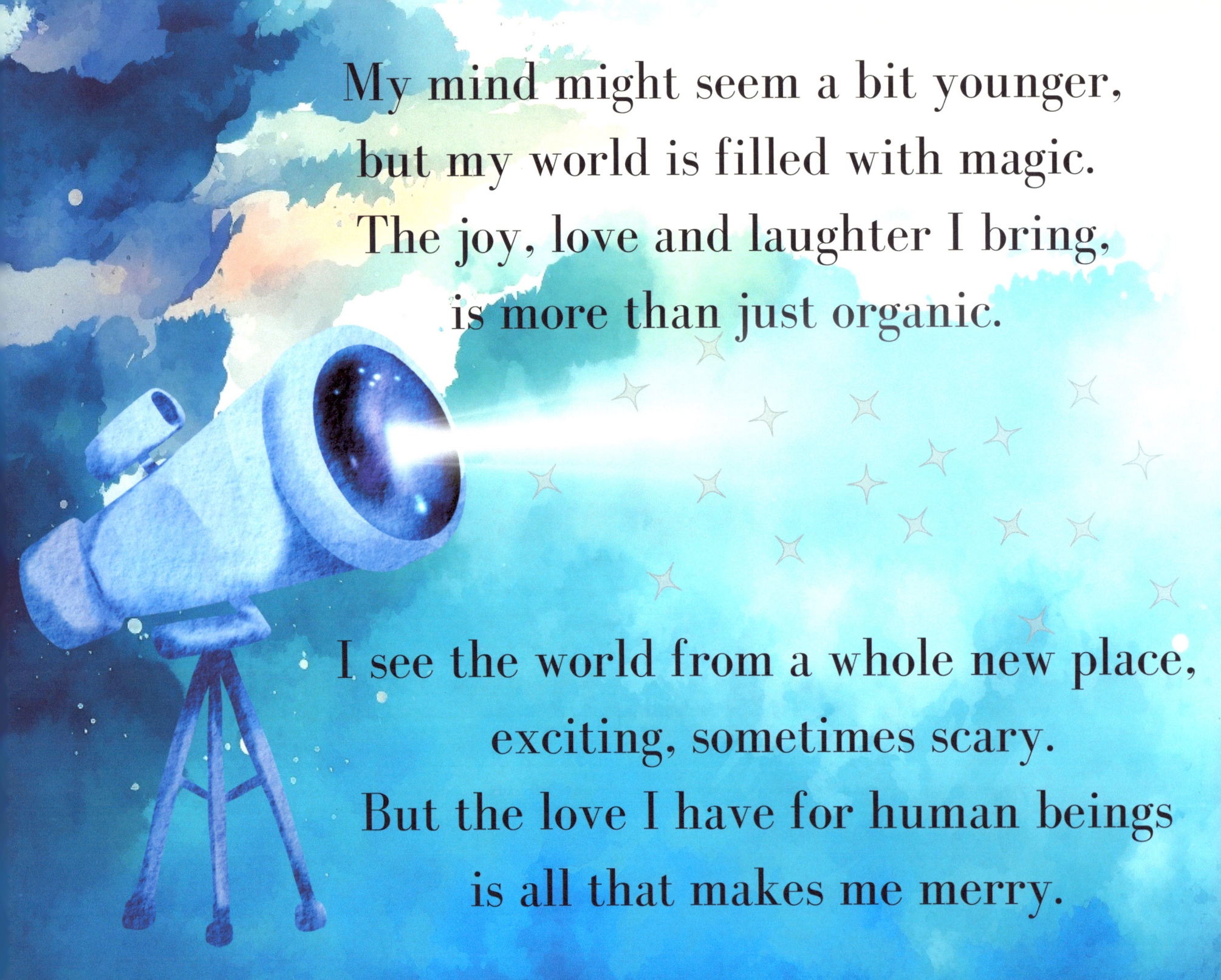

My mind might seem a bit younger,
but my world is filled with magic.
The joy, love and laughter I bring,
is more than just organic.

I see the world from a whole new place,
exciting, sometimes scary.
But the love I have for human beings
is all that makes me merry.

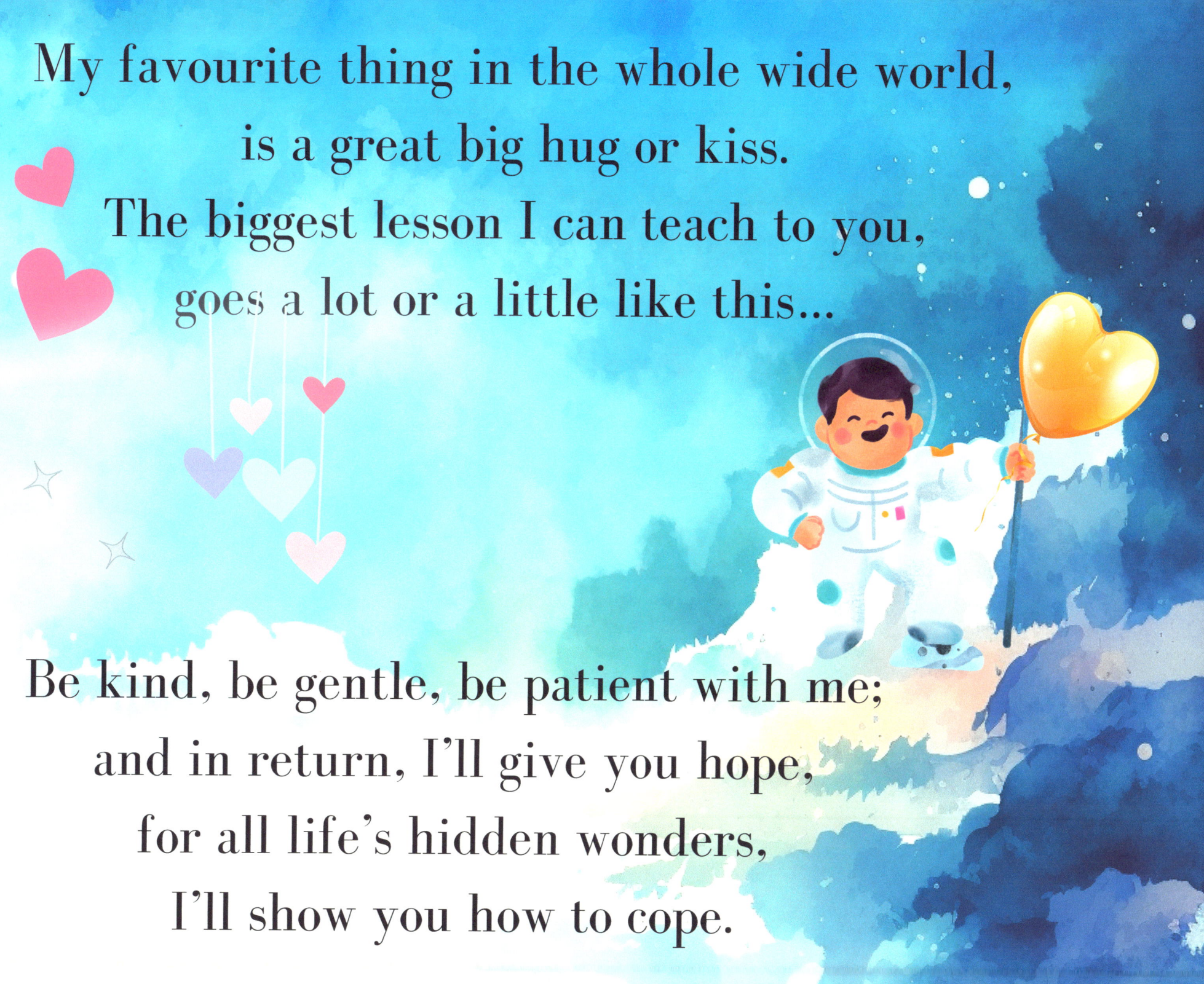

My favourite thing in the whole wide world,
is a great big hug or kiss.
The biggest lesson I can teach to you,
goes a lot or a little like this...

Be kind, be gentle, be patient with me;
and in return, I'll give you hope,
for all life's hidden wonders,
I'll show you how to cope.

To you I might look a little different,
to you I might act a little odd;
but you see I am the imperfectly perfect,
most special child from God.

I am my own person,
my very own me.
I AM THE BIGGEST SUPERSTAR
I know, special and unique.

Hi, my name is Pauly,
I've learned I have Cerebral Palsy.
What have I learned about me?
Well, I have special superpowers,
let me help you see.

I know I am a genius,
my mind is very bright.
But sometimes I struggle a bit with my body,
catching up with my insight.

I love to push my boundaries
in everything I do;
because I know deep down in my big big heart,
I'm really a lot like you.

I can be a little headstrong,
but I can also be super brave.
I can get overstimulated,
but my senses are like waves.

I can be a little quiet,
antisocial they might say;
but every time I express myself,
I shine in every way.

To you I might look a little different,
to you I might act a little odd;
but you see I am the imperfectly perfect,
most special child from God.

I am my own person,
my very own me.
I AM THE BIGGEST SUPERSTAR
I know, special and unique.

Remember everyone is different,
and everyone is unique.
We are all in some big way

SUPERSTARS!

at our very peak.

Please be kind to everything,
be kind to everyone.
You never know how someone feels,
we're all part of the same sun.

Alex Webster is a South African born mom, wife, kinesiologist and artist who has a passion for everything creative.

She began her writing journey with creating personalised children's books for family friends, which ignited a passion into the world of graphic design and creative writing. Having a kinesiology background, she has a vast understanding of the underlying emotions connected to the mind, body and soul.

"Every child is born imperfectly perfect to make this world a better place. May we learn to embrace all the love they give, and all the lessons they teach us."
- Alex Webster

Printed in the USA
CPSIA information can be obtained
at www.ICGtesting.com
LVHW061633290923
759528LV00005B/165